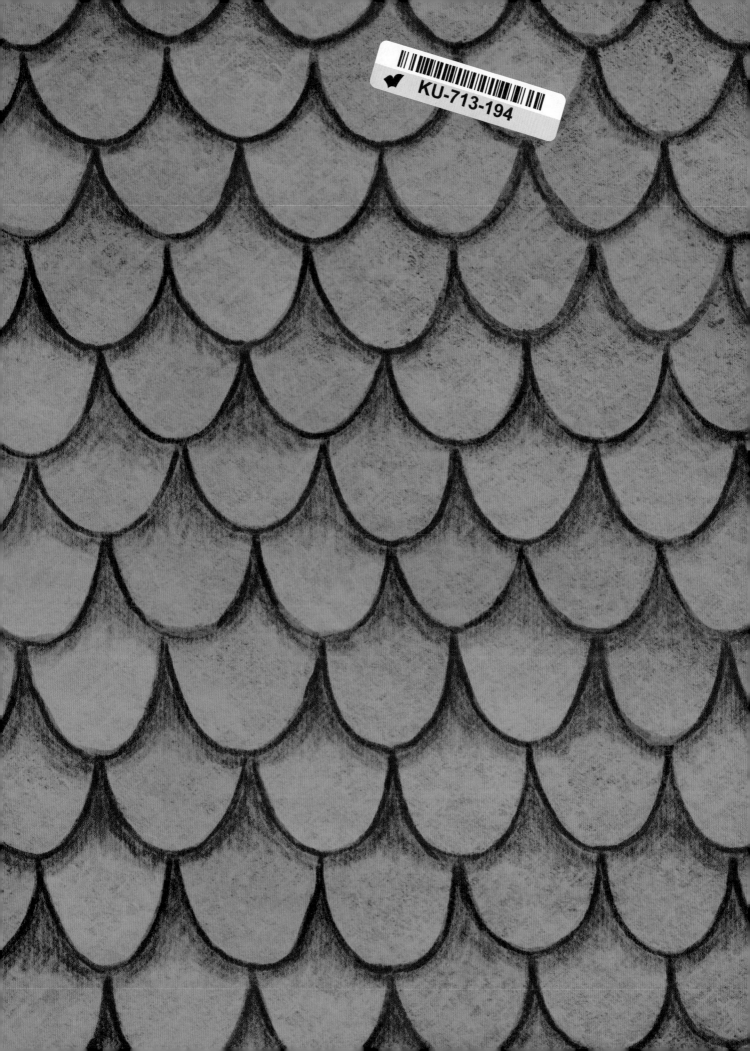

FOR MY MOM

SIMON & SCHUSTER BOOKS FOR YOUNG READERS
An imprint of Simon & Schuster Children's Publishing Division
1230 Avenue of the Americas, New York, New York 10020
© 2021 by Alex Willan • Book design by Chloë Foglia and
Alex Willan © 2021 by Simon & Schuster, Inc. • All rights reserved,
including the right of reproduction in whole or in part in any form.
SIMON & SCHUSTER BOOKS FOR YOUNG READERS
and related marks are trademarks of Simon & Schuster, Inc.
For information about special discounts for bulk purchases, please
contact Simon & Schuster Special Sales at 1-866-506-1949 or
business@simonandschuster.com.
The Simon & Schuster Speakers Bureau can bring authors to your
live event. For more information or to book an event, contact the
Simon & Schuster Speakers Bureau at 1-866-248-3049 or visit our
website at www.simonspeakers.com.
The text for this book was set in Rockwell.
The illustrations for this book were rendered digitally.
Manufactured in China • 0621 SCP • First Edition
10 9 8 7 6 5 4 3 2 1
Library of Congress Cataloging-in-Publication Data
Names: Willan, Alex, author, illustrator.
Title: Dragons are the worst! / Alex Willan.
Description: First edition. | New York : Simon & Schuster Books for Young Readers,
[2021] | Audience: Ages 4-8. | Audience: Grades K-1. | Summary: Disgruntled
Gilbert the Goblin argues that dragons are terrible and not nearly as frightening
as he is, but perspectives change when knights arrive to capture a dragon.
Identifiers: LCCN 2020055514 | ISBN 9781534485112 (hardcover) | ISBN 9781534485129 (ebook)
Subjects: CYAC: Goblins—Fiction. | Dragons—Fiction. | Humorous stories.
Classification: LCC PZ7.1.W545 Dr 2021 | DDC [E]—dc23
LC record available at https://lccn.loc.gov/2020055514

DRAGONS
ARE
THE
WORST!

BY
ALEX WILLAN

Simon & Schuster Books for Young Readers
NEW YORK LONDON TORONTO SYDNEY NEW DELHI

You know, we goblins have been around for ages. There was a time when our magical misdeeds were taken seriously, even feared.

But lately it seems like everyone is only concerned about one thing . . .

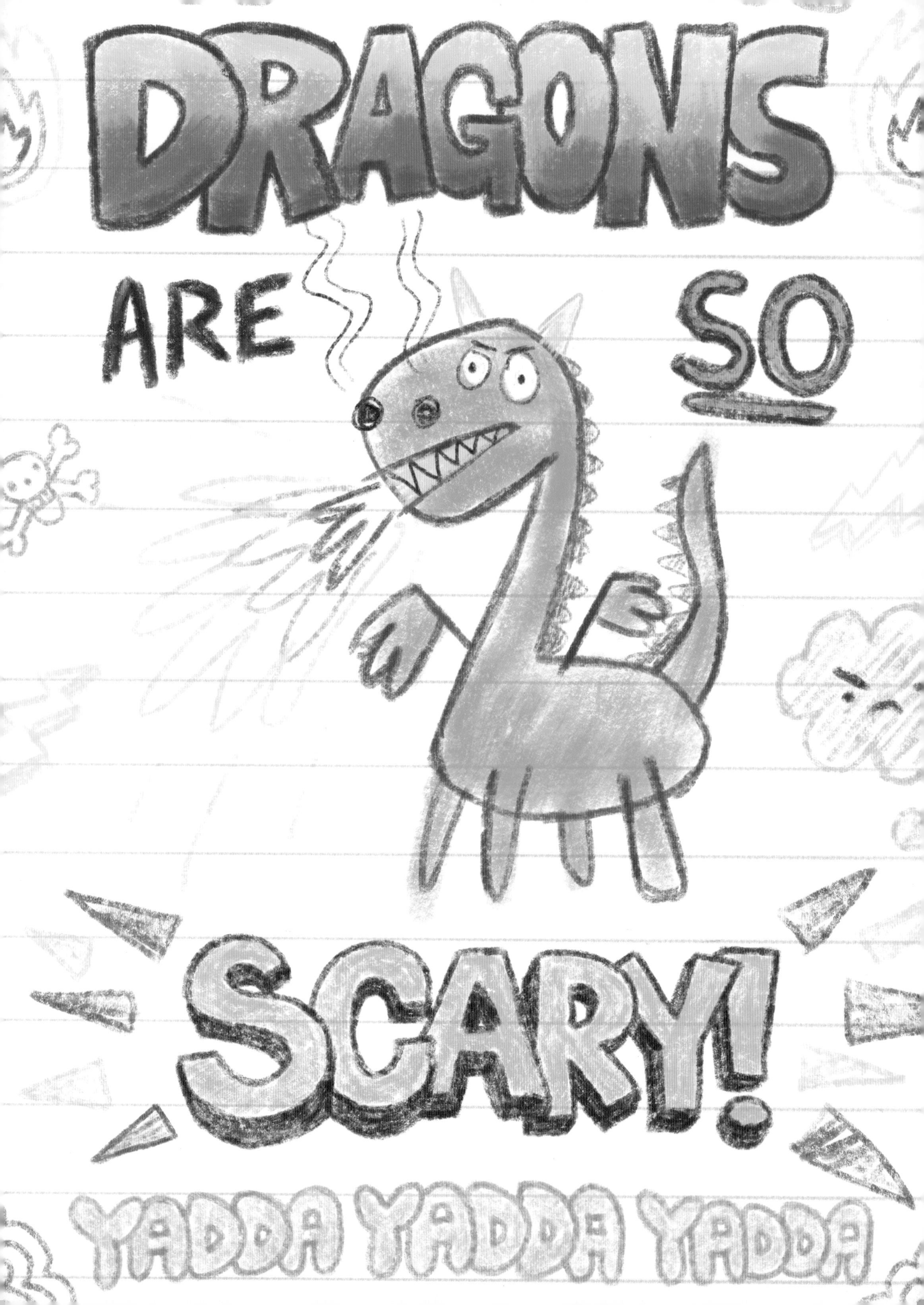
DRAGONS
ARE SO
SCARY!
YADDA YADDA YADDA

GOBLINS

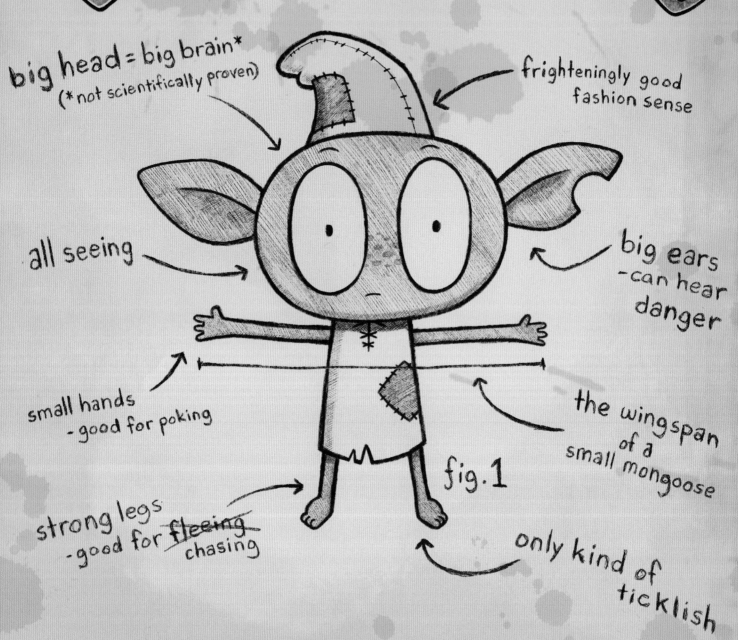

big head = big brain*
(*not scientifically proven)

frighteningly good fashion sense

all seeing

big ears
-can hear danger

small hands
- good for poking

the wingspan of a small mongoose

strong legs
-good for ~~fleeing~~ chasing

fig.1

only kind of ticklish

fig.2

fig.3

I know spells that can make your shoelaces come untied,

fig.4

fig.5

I can turn candy into spiders,

and I've perfected my terrifying pigeon costume. . . .

But does anyone run in fear from *my* magical might?

When you think about it, dragons aren't even that scary. Sure, they can breathe fire, but all that hot breath makes eating ice cream nearly impossible.

Having all those sharp teeth just means it takes forever to floss. . . .

And good luck finding a hat that fits when you have big spiky horns.

And so what if dragons can soar through the skies. . . .

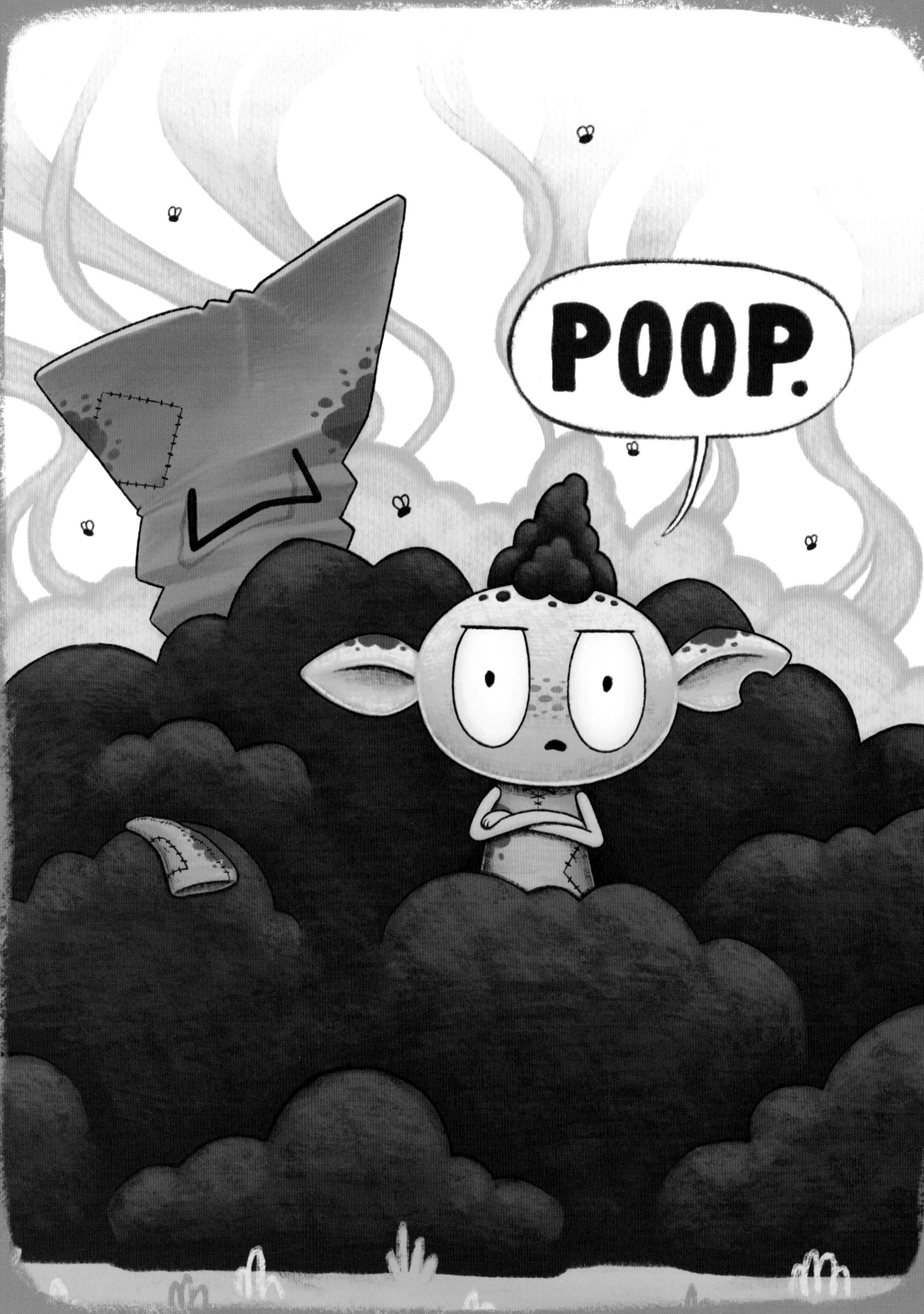
POOP.

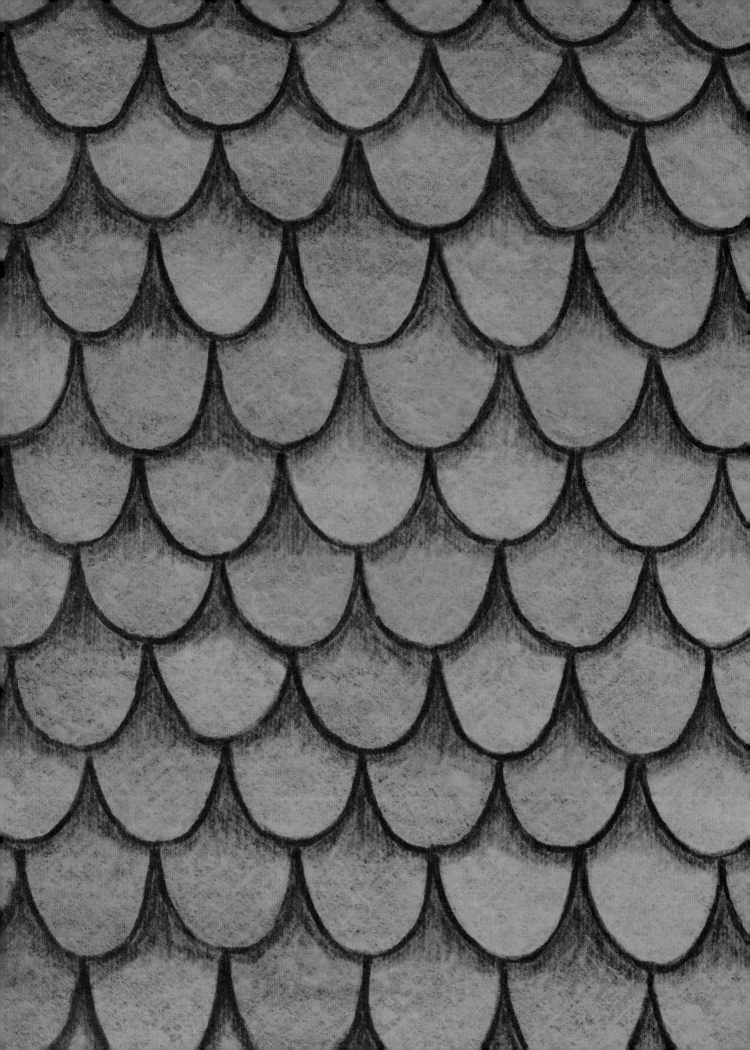